The Day My Father Became a Bush

Joke van Leeuwen

Also by Joke van Leeuwen

Eep! (Gecko Press)

The Day
My Father
Became
a Bush

Joke van Leeuwen

GECKO PRESS

This edition first published in 2013 by Gecko Press
PO Box 9335, Marion Square, Wellington 6141, New Zealand
info@geckopress.com

Copyright text and illustrations © 2010 by Joke van Leeuwen,
Amsterdam, Em. Querido's Uitgeverij B.V.
Original title: *Toen mijn vader een struik werd*

English language edition © Gecko Press Ltd 2013
Translation © Bill Nagelkerke 2013

First American edition published in 2014 by Gecko Press USA,
an imprint of Gecko Press Ltd.
Distributed in the United States and Canada by
Lerner Publishing Group, Inc.
241 First Avenue North
Minneapolis, MN 55401 USA
www.lernerbooks.com
A catalog record for this book is available from the US Library
of Congress.

Edited by Penelope Todd
Typeset by Book Design, New Zealand
Cover design by Spencer Levine
Printed by Everbest, China

ISBN hardback (USA): 978-1-877579-48-6
ISBN paperback: 978-1-877579-16-5

This book was published with the support
of the Dutch Foundation for Literature.

N ederlands
letterenfonds
dutch foundation
for literature

For more curiously good books, visit www.geckopress.com

1

When my father became a bush we were living somewhere else.

At the time I never thought of it as somewhere else. Somewhere else was anywhere except where we lived.

Everyone used to pronounce my name easily. Where I live now, no one can. They can't say the letter *k*. The first person who tried pronouncing my name got his tongue in a twist.

These days I call myself Toda. Those are the last four letters of my long first name, which has four *k*'s in it.

I used to live with my dad in a small city. That city was big enough for me.

My mother didn't live with us. I didn't really know her very well. I had a photo of her smiling.

Sometimes I talked to her on the phone, but it was hard to know what to say. She said she missed me but I wondered why she never came to visit. Dad told me that she'd left just before I turned one. And not because of me, he said, but because she couldn't cope anymore. He didn't say what it was she couldn't cope with. But then I never asked.

Before my father turned into a bush he was a pastry chef. He got up at four o'clock every morning to bake twenty different sorts of pastries and three kinds of cake.

During the day they were sold and eaten, every one of them. Next morning he'd get up at four again to bake twenty different sorts of pastries and three kinds of cake. He told me never to become a baker. I'd be better off selling things that weren't gobbled up right away. His baking smelled scrumptious though.

One evening he sat me on his lap and told me that people were in no hurry to buy pastries anymore. Things were going badly in our country. There was fighting in the south between one side and another. He said the fighting hadn't reached us yet, but if things carried on this way then it could start up here as well. He told me that Gran was coming to stay with me for a while. He had to go and help defend one side against the other even though he had friends who were on the other side. He had no choice, he said, no matter how much he'd rather make pastries.

He showed me a thin, dark green book. It was called *What Every Soldier Needs to Know*.

One chapter was all about camouflage. I didn't know that word then.

"Camouflage," said my father, "is when you make yourself unrecognizable. You have to be able to disguise yourself."

There was a picture in the book of a soldier who had disguised himself as a bush.

On another page were pictures of a whole lot of military decorations. These were sewn onto a uniform to show how good someone was at something. Whoever made those decorations was very good at sewing. Ordinary soldiers' decorations were plain but generals' ones were sewn with gold thread.

When my father left, my grandmother arrived. She put the sugar bowl in the wrong place and smothered the sofa with a throw blanket. I told her that my father had to dress up as a bush.

He would only do that if he was in a forest, she said,

not in the middle of a city or somewhere like that. If you sat down in the middle of the street disguised as a bush, you'd only draw attention to yourself.

I wondered how he could camouflage himself in a city. Perhaps he'd have to pretend to be a mailbox or a parked car. Or a tree on the footpath.

At school I'd been a tree once, but I wasn't allowed to have real branches or leaves. It was hard not to look like a person. My arms pointed at the ceiling, like two thick branches with ten twigs at the ends. To make it seem more real I said, "Rustle, rustle."

A girl from my class was amazingly good at imitating animals and things. But even she still looked like herself.

swan   sugar bowl

My father would be allowed to use real branches and leaves. I'd seen that in the dark green book. That way the enemy wouldn't be able to spot him. They'd think, that's a bush. Or they'd walk right past him and think nothing of it. Because when you walk past a bush you don't usually stop to think, that's a bush. At least the enemy wasn't likely to shoot at a bush. In fact, if my father camouflaged himself really well, even the birds might not notice him. They might build a nest on his head and sit in it, hatching their eggs.

But what if the enemy also had a book that explained how to camouflage themselves? And what if they all disguised themselves as bushes? How would anyone know who belonged to which side?

I thought a lot about these things, but I didn't talk about them with my grandmother even though she'd lived through a war and survived.

She hugged me and said, "Your father's a grown man now but he'll always be my son."

And then she looked out the window into the street as if she expected him back at any second.

2

My grandmother was patient. Sometimes she took the hairpins out of her long hair and let me arrange it in different styles.

She'd sit still on the
sofa with her eyes closed.
Sometimes she complained
that I was pulling too hard and
she said she would quite like to
have some hair left in ten years'
time. When I'd finished, she
laughed at herself in the mirror.

But afterwards she always put her hair back the way it had been.

At night all the hairpins lay in a row on her bedside table and she let her hair spread over the pillow. I saw it one night when I crept into bed beside her. I was too scared to stay in my own bed. I heard loud blasts outside and saw lights flare across the wallpaper. My gran said that the war had reached us and that we would be safer sleeping down below in the bakery now. We took the duvet with us and a couple of pillows. Downstairs, Gran spread the throw from the sofa on the floor under the workbench. It looked as if it had been snowing lightly in the night but it was only flour lying on the floor.

The oven door stood open like a big, black eye. Just below the ceiling, two small windows faced the street. When it grew light outside you could see the shoes of people walking past. The garden was below street level. When the heat of the oven made my father too hot, he could slip out the side door for a stroll.

My gran tried singing me a song. Her voice wobbled. She sang an old-fashioned song about grass and trees.

I asked when all the blasting would stop, but she didn't know.

"Perhaps if it starts pouring with rain," I said, "then they'll go inside."

I hoped it would start pouring.

I'm sure I lay awake for another hour.

Finally the blasting stopped and I fell asleep.

It was daylight when we opened our eyes again. My gran was so stiff from lying on the hard, cold floor that she could hardly get up.

During breakfast she muttered to the marmalade jar that no one could behave normally anymore.

She must have been thinking about my father because he was her son.

I went back to thinking about camouflage. I wished I could disguise myself so that the enemy would never guess where I was. No one would be able to give me away either. If the enemy asked, people would say, "Her? We've got no idea where she is. We've even forgotten what she looks like."

Eventually they would forget about me altogether. I'd stay hidden, forever. No one would even come to tell me, "The coast is clear. It's safe to come out now."

I wasn't allowed to go outside. I noticed Gran trying to phone someone but our telephone didn't work. She said she would go out instead to arrange a few things. I had to stay at home and not let anyone in.

Her face was very tense. It would crack if she smiled.

After she left, I sat on the sofa. It was no longer being suffocated by the throw.

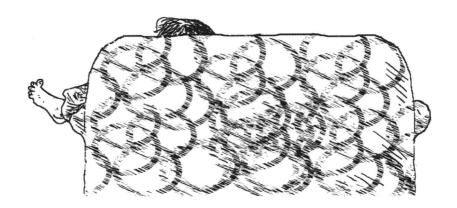

From now on there would be no more ordinary days for doing ordinary things. And no more ordinary nights of sleeping and waking. I stayed on the sofa for two whole hours, desperate to do something ordinary. Then the doorbell rang. I was frozen with fear. It might be the enemy at the door.

The bell rang and rang as if the enemy knew I was inside, even though I pretended I wasn't. Sometimes I managed to count to four before it rang again.

I couldn't just stay on the sofa.

Perhaps I should barricade the front door. But then Gran wouldn't be able to get back inside when she came home.

I tiptoed out into the hall. The door was still shut. I could lock it. It had two strong locks.

As I was wondering whether or not to, someone called through the mail slot, "For goodness sake, open the door!"

Not the enemy. It was Gran!

"Didn't you hear me calling?" she said, once she was inside. "I forgot to take the key with me."

"You told me not to open the door."

"Yes, that's true."

The hairpins were no longer in her hair.

I had to go back and sit on the sofa. Gran had something to tell me.

She said I couldn't stay here. Things had become too dangerous. And she couldn't let anything bad happen to me because I was her grandchild.

She said she had contacted my mother. Across the border, where my mother lived, there was no war. It would be best if I went there. My mother would welcome me with open arms.

"But I'd rather be with Dad," I said.

My gran knew that already. But it would only be for a while, she said. When the danger was over, I could come back.

I asked if that meant she wasn't coming with me.

"No, I can't," Gran said. She had to look after the house otherwise someone else would come and live in it. They would take everything that belonged to my father.

But there was no need for me to worry about her. She had lived through one war already.

"There aren't any earthquakes or floods where I'm going, are there?" I asked. "I might as well stay home otherwise."

No, there weren't any of those, my gran said. And this was the best thing to do in the circumstances.

I could tell she would have preferred other circumstances. But they weren't to be.

"You won't be on your own," Gran said. "They promised me that. Someone will be with you the whole way. And you're not the only one. Other children are being sent away to safety, too. A bus is leaving the day after tomorrow."

We sat next to each other for a while, not saying anything. Then Gran pulled me close and wrapped me in her arms as if she was never going to let me go. I could hardly breathe.

3

Whatever I took with me had to fit inside my shoulder bag. I managed to squeeze in four pairs of underwear, two T-shirts, one pair of jeans, a sweater, my toiletries bag, one packet of cookies, a bottle of water, a notebook, and a pen. Everything else I had to leave behind. Gran said she would take good care of it all.

In the notebook, she wrote down my mother's address and glued a photo of her beside it. She also stuck in a photo of my father. And a photocopy of his passport which had my name in it.

She didn't have a photo of herself so she drew a picture of her face, but she wasn't much good at drawing. She crossed herself out three times.

"You'll just have to remember what I look like," she said.

Together we made a list of all the other things I had to remember.

List

- What the twenty different kinds of pastries looked like and how they tasted.
- How we laughed when we laughed.
- Gran's wobbly way of singing.
- Dad's lap.
- All the cuddles I've ever had since I was three.
- The music box that came from Dad's grandmother and which Gran is going to look after for me.
- My best dress and my gold ring.
- My two best friends.
- The low wall in the street where we always used to sit.

We arranged everything in my bag to make it as easy as possible to carry. My gran sewed a secret pocket into the inside of my jeans. She stuffed as much money into it as she could. The people organizing the bus had said I wouldn't need to pay for anything during the trip. But just in case, she said.

Outside the sun carried on shining as if nothing was wrong.

I knew that tomorrow would come, and the next day, but I couldn't think further ahead than that.

The bus was waiting under leaf-laden trees. It looked as if it had tried to camouflage itself, too.

"Try to think of this as a kind of vacation," said my gran. But it didn't look like much of a vacation since nearly everyone was crying. We were, too. The only ones not crying were the bus driver and the two women who were going to look after us on the journey.

I didn't know any of the other children. They were all about my age. I wondered if children older and younger than us were going in other buses. And all the old people in an old people's bus. I thought that zoo animals should be taken to safety, too, since they couldn't escape from their enclosures by themselves.

As the bus slowly pulled away from under the trees my gran forgot to wave. She just stood and stared at me until I couldn't see her anymore. It was as if she wanted time to stand still and thought it might help if she stood still herself. She looked suddenly older. As the bus drove on, I kept thinking about that last glimpse of her. I felt homesick. It was like a nagging ache that I couldn't rub away.

I didn't talk to the other children.

I looked out the window.

The first houses we drove past had been destroyed, but a little further on they were still whole. The war hadn't reached here yet. I saw sheep grazing peacefully on the foothills. They had no idea what people were up to.

We stopped once at the edge of a forest. Whoever needed to go to the bathroom had to hide behind scrappy bushes between rows of thin trees. The ground was littered with dead branches. When I looked up I saw a green roof shutting out the sun. I hoped my father wasn't having to hide in this sort of a forest.

We drove for four hours before stopping in the village where we were going to stay the night. It was a village without war and without stores. It had almost nothing.

"Public Welfare" was written in faded letters on the only big building. I asked one of the women what the words meant. She said that the things that happened in the building were of public importance. But she didn't say what those things were.

We went through an imposing door into a wide hallway. The walls were painted dirty green and looked as if they were covered in pimples. It was the ugliest green I'd ever seen.

We went past seven doors. Behind the eighth was a room with a high ceiling. It was jam-packed with beds. You could tell they didn't really belong there.

Thick, dark brown curtains hung in the windows. They had already been closed even though it wasn't dark yet outside. Round lamps hung from the ceilings. There were sheets on the beds, and blankets that looked as if they would be very scratchy.

We each had to pick a bed. Some children wanted to sleep next to one another.

I put my bag on a bed close to the door.

Then a man came in. He said that we were welcome

here for the night, and that we would continue our journey the following day.

Other buses would be arriving tomorrow, he said, carrying a new lot of people. For now, we had to sit quietly on our beds. We'd get something to eat in an hour or so.

The man left. He must have worked for the Public Welfare.

I sat on my bed, staring down at my shoes. I wasn't planning to take them off tonight. If the war suddenly reached the town I needed to be able to get away and hide somewhere.

After a while I heard voices in the hall. They came closer, and before I knew what was happening the room was full of other children and mothers. The mothers pointed us out and the children sniveled and handed us each a book or a stuffed animal or a toy car. The books looked well read, the stuffed animals were grubby, and the little cars were scuffed. The mothers said that their children had decided, all by themselves, to give us these presents because things were so difficult for us.

When everything had been handed out and looked at, one of the mothers said to us, "I imagine you're very happy with them." And another said, "Don't forget to say thank you."

So we all said thank you. Some of the mothers thought it wasn't good enough. We had to say it together, clearly.

So we said, all together, "Thank you!"

No, another mother said we must try once more, louder.

We all yelled, "THANK YOU!"

"Not like that," said yet another mother. "You have to really mean it."

A girl with pigtails was holding a stuffed monster in her hands.

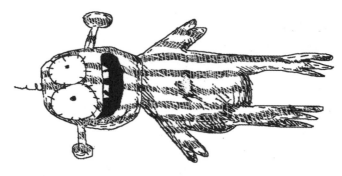

"I don't actually like it very much," she said carefully.

"Is that what we get?" asked the mother of the boy who had given her the monster. "How's that for ingratitude?"

The other mothers joined in. They all looked very indignant.

"You don't deserve to get anything at all. Give it back."

The girl was too scared to look at the mothers. As she laid the monster at the end of her bed, she looked down at her knees instead.

The boy who had given it to her snatched it back and clutched it tight.

The other children who had given presents started talking all at once, "That's not fair! We've given things and he hasn't! We want ours back, too!"

They reached across the beds and grabbed at the toys. But some of us clung onto our presents and yelled, "No, you've already given it! It's too late! It's mine now. Mine! Mine!"

The two sides fought each other. They punched one another in the stomach. They pulled apart the stuffed animals and crashed the cars onto the floor. The blankets slid off the beds and the sheets got all messed up.

The mothers tried to drag their children away and herd them towards the door.

"She started it!" they shouted, pointing at the girl with the pigtails who was still staring down at her knees.

"Ungrateful children," growled the last mother to leave as she closed the door behind her. "You should go back to where you came from."

I sat on my bed and looked around the room. Yes, I thought, I'd love to go back to where I came from. But I can't.

The room had grown very quiet.

The only sound came from the girl with the pigtails. She muttered: "I didn't even want it…didn't want it."

KNIGHT-TIME TALES

4

We had to go to bed.

I kept my clothes and shoes on and crept under the scratchy blankets so no one could see that I wasn't in pajamas.

Some children cried and called for their mothers. Someone would go to the beds of the loudest criers and say, "Hush now."

I fell asleep. In my dream at least fifty people came into our house insisting that they were going to live there.

My grandmother couldn't stop them.

She kept saying, "Hey, you can't just do that."

The people took over our house. They lay down on the floor and the sofa, in the hallway and on the kitchen table.

When I woke up, I had no idea what the time was. A dim light bulb had been left on in the room. It was just bright enough to show where the beds and the door were.

Because I had to go to the bathroom, I crept into the hall. I knew that there was another smaller hallway behind the third door on the left. That's where the bathroom was.

I ran my hands over the pimply wall until I found the light switch. Once I'd gone I put the lid of the toilet down and stood on it. That way I could look outside.

I saw stars in the sky. I saw a half moon. And a lone tree in an empty field. Nothing moved.

I wondered if my father was asleep somewhere under a different tree, camouflaged as a chopped-down bush.

I heard voices. They were coming from behind another door. The voices sounded a bit like my

grandmother's. Perhaps a busload of grandmothers had arrived and mine was one of them. She'd decided to come because it was too dangerous to stay at home, even though she'd made it through one war already.

Carefully I peeked round the edge of the door. I saw a big, high room with a whole lot of armchairs. Sitting in the chairs were women who were all nearly old, or actually old.

They saw me.

I went a bit closer and asked, "Do you know if my grandmother is here somewhere?"

"Did she come on the bus?" asked the one nearest to me.

"She stayed to look after our house," I said.

"Then she won't be here," the near one said. "Because we came by bus. Even earlier than you. But you were given the beds and we had to sleep in the chairs."

She took hold of me and sat me on her lap.

"*We're* here," she said.

"Now it's my turn," said the woman beside her. She pulled me over and sat me on *her* lap. And so it kept going. They moved me from lap to lap. Because I was still a bit sleepy, I let them. Also, I could see that it made them happy.

Every lap was different. Some were wide and rocked like a boat. Some were very soft, although you couldn't sink all the way in because a stomach got in the way. Some were hard and bony, and there was even one I nearly fell right through.

Once I'd tried out all the laps they put me down again.

"Now," they said. "Who are you going to choose?"

I didn't know what they meant. Had this been a "best lap" competition?

"Who are you going to choose as a stand-in grandmother?" they asked.

"I already have a perfectly good grandmother," I said. "The one who's looking after our house."

"But you're not going to see her for a while," said the woman with the widest lap.

"I'll see her when things get back to normal at home."

"Then you might as well have a temporary grandmother," said the one with the bony lap. "Just tell us whose adopted grandchild you want to be."

"But I'm not adopted," I said. "I'm real."

"Of course you are! And adopted children are real as well," cried the woman with the lap that rocked the most.

She pinched my skin.

"Does your mother feed you enough red meat?"

"I've never lived with my mother," I said.

"Dear child, then you're allowed *two* temporary grandmothers."

I suddenly realized that their mouths were smiling but their eyes weren't.

"Don't you have any grandchildren of your own?" I asked.

"Of course," said the bony-lap woman. "But mine live a thousand miles away."

"And mine at least ten thousand miles," said the one next to her.

"And mine," said the woman with the smallest lap, "mine live on the other side of the world and speak a different language."

"Oh," I said.

And then they took turns telling me why I should let them be my stand-in grandmother for a while.

"I can teach you some lovely old songs," said the first.

"And I can teach you unforgettable tongue twisters," said the second.

*She sells seashells
by the seashore.*

"And I can teach you some great tricks," said the third. She showed me a trick immediately. I had to wrap my hand around hers.

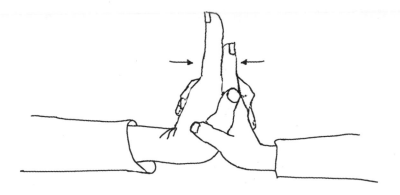

Our index fingers made a tower. I had to rub the tower
with the thumb and first finger of my other hand.

"Strange, isn't it," she said. "It feels as if your finger
is half dead."

"I can teach you to whistle," said the fourth.

"I can do that already," I said.

"Well then, I'll teach you something else."

"No, no," said the fifth. "It's my turn now. You've
had yours."

"Who says?" said the fourth.

"Those are the rules," said the fifth.

"I didn't know there were rules," the fourth one
said angrily.

Then they all chimed in. One said that the fourth
woman should be allowed to say what else she could
teach me. Another said the fifth woman had been
right about rules otherwise they'd never get anywhere.
Another insisted that they'd both had their turn and
now they should shut up.

All the stand-in grandmothers talked over the

top of one another. They were so busy telling each other what they should and shouldn't think that they stopped taking any notice of me.

I thought about my gran who was far away. I definitely didn't want any other grandmother.

So I slipped back through the door, into the hallway.

And no one came after me.

5

I dreamt I took the train back home. There were
grandmothers on board, as well as dogs, and bakers
with flour on their hands. There were also lots of
animals from the zoo. A lion lay quietly next to a
lamb, and a bear with a mouse on his head took up
two seats. When I got home, I saw my father standing
in the kitchen. Branches sprouted from his body. He
had holes in his clothes where they poked through.
The branches were all bare. In his body it was winter.

I wanted to tidy up his hair but when I touched it,
it fell out of his head. He went completely bald. I got
a terrible shock and said there was nothing I could do
about it. My father said, Hush now, hush now.

And then I woke up to find that the day had begun.

We had to go and stand in the wide hallway, in our
underwear.

At school we'd once had to wait in an empty classroom, dressed like that. A doctor had used a popsicle stick to look down our throats. He'd pinched our skin here and there and asked if we got breakfast at home. I didn't like being nearly naked when I should be dressed. It was like going swimming in a skirt or walking across the street in pajamas.

We took turns going around the corner into the smaller hallway by the bathroom. The two women looking after us were there in big aprons.

"Hurry up," they said.

One washed me very quickly while the other dried me much too roughly. They spoke to each other in serious voices, mostly about things I couldn't make out because the towel was scouring my ears. The only thing I heard properly was, "You don't want to know."

After that we had to get dressed in our room and we were given two cheese sandwiches and a small cup of juice. As soon as we had finished we had to line up again with our luggage in the big hallway.

No one spoke. We didn't know what was going to happen today. I thought about my grandmother having breakfast by herself, muttering at the marmalade jar. She might have had to sleep down in the bakery again and, like me, would have decided it was better to sleep with her clothes on. She had to look after the whole house and stop anyone from coming inside yelling, "I'm going to live here now, too!" Hopefully she'd be strong enough to send someone like that packing. But she had such saggy skin on her arms, the muscles under it were bound to be weak as well.

The man who had welcomed us the day before was standing in front of us, looking down the line. He took a map from under his arm and shook it open.

"Today we're going to split you up," he said.

One girl started to cry because she thought he meant we were going to be taken apart, like a doll. But at least you can put a doll put back together again.

"This is what's happening," said the man. "Some children have a place to go to, other children don't. We're going to divide you into three groups. Group one will wait in the bedroom. Those are the children who have an address on the other side of the border. They'll be taken to another town where they'll be met by people who know how to get them across the border. Group two will go and stand by the front door. Those are the children who have an address nearby. They'll be taken there as soon as possible. Group three are the children who have no address to go to. They'll stay standing where they are. For the time being they'll be placed with a family, but they won't have a choice about which family. The fact is that some families would rather take in a girl with long hair than a boy with a loud voice. You'll have to accept that."

That gave us a shock. Even those of us with somewhere to go wondered what sort of things those families might find wrong with us.

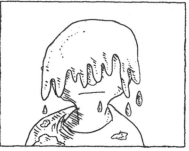

Licking up our snot because we didn't have a hanky.

Not understanding something and doing it the wrong way.

Not knowing our thirteen-times table by heart.

Singing songs they didn't like.

Swinging our legs under the table.

Dropping and breaking something.

Forgetting to wipe our feet.

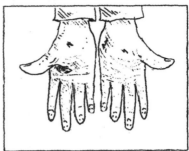

Forgetting to wash our hands before we ate.

Not saying "thank you" often enough.

Not finishing our food because we felt full.

Accidentally farting when we were supposed to be quiet.

Not being able to remember an important word.

There were so many reasons why no one would want us.

I was the only one who had to wait in the bedroom. Obviously none of the other children knew anyone who lived on the other side of the border. It was strange to sit there waiting in a sea of beds, like someone drowning.

6

I had to get into a big old car that stank of cigarettes and dog. The two women and the man with the map waved me off. I was glad the women wouldn't be washing me again. They had nearly scrubbed the ears off my head.

The driver didn't say anything. He drove for hours through forests and villages, past lonely farms and astonished-looking cows. He stopped a couple of times to pick up other people. Two women climbed in first, then later on a man and a boy joined us. It was crowded in the car. I was squeezed up against the window. The man's clothes smelled of sweat.

The third time the driver stopped, we were in the middle of nowhere. He parked the car in the shade of an enormous tree and spoke for the first time.

"You have to pay," he said, "otherwise you won't be taken across the border."

Everyone climbed out. The others produced money which they handed over to the driver.

When they had all paid, he told me I had to pay as well.

"Where's your money?" he asked. "In the hem of your T-shirt? In the false bottom of your bag? If you don't hand it over, I'll search until I find it."

I was very scared when he said that. I thought he might tear my bag and my clothes or leave me behind if I didn't pay.

But if I did, my secret pocket wouldn't be secret any more.

I turned my back to him, unzipped my pants, and took all the money out of the secret pocket. Then I zipped them up again and turned around.

"This is all I've got," I said, handing over the money. I'd never had so much money before. And now I had none left.

"It's not enough," he said.

I tried not to burst into tears.

"I can pay the extra with cookies," I sniffed.

The other people got angry with the driver. He shouldn't treat a child like that, they said. But he hissed at them to shut up or else he'd leave us right here to make our own way to the border. If we could.

We shut up. But we carried on talking with our eyes and hands without a word being spoken.

In the end, I was allowed to go with them. Possibly we were already close to the border. I'd never been to a border before and had no idea what one looked like. Was it a line drawn on the ground or a wall? Or a hedge of barbed wire?

Or perhaps it was just a sign with both ends pointing to different countries.

Would there be people in uniform who'd ask, "And where are *you* going?"

I suddenly remembered my father telling me once that there was a "no-man's land" between countries. Did that mean no one was allowed to live there? Or perhaps people could live there, but no one was in charge. Or, if you lived there, you couldn't have a name.

Late in the afternoon, the car stopped just outside a town. I saw a long wall with doors in it that ran the whole length of the street. Each door had a number on it.

The driver said we could go through door number seven and wait inside. In the middle of the night, someone would collect us and take us across the border. We mustn't tell anybody where we were going.

He drove away without saying goodbye.

The door of number seven opened into a concrete shed. Inside there were only two mattresses. There was nothing to eat or drink. I had no money left to buy anything, and the shops would all be closed anyway.

All I had was a couple of cookies and a little bit of water.

The women immediately took over the mattresses. There was no space left on them for the man and the boy or for me.

"Do we really have to stay here until the middle of the night?" the boy asked.

"I don't think so," said the man. "As long as we're not away too long and no one sees us coming or going. The best way to be inconspicuous is to go for a walk and act as if we belong here."

The man peered around the shed door to make sure the coast was clear. Then he and the boy slipped outside.

I looked at the women. They ignored me. They lay on the mattresses, sighing heavily. If I stayed with them for hours in this dark hole, I'd probably end up sighing like them. A sigh for my father. A sigh for my grandmother. A sigh for all the things I hadn't been able to take with me. A sigh for the money I no longer had. A sigh for the bakery that used to smell so lovely. A sigh because I knew nothing and nobody anymore.

Since the man had said it was okay to go outside, I decided I might as well. So I sneaked out onto the street as inconspicuously as I could even though my bag, draped over my shoulder, was a bit too big for someone pretending to belong there and just going out for a stroll.

I was hungry. My tummy rumbled.

When I reached the street corner, I turned around. I wanted to see how the street looked so I'd remember it on the way back. On one side, the numbered wall came to an end. On the other side was a hedge that seemed to be made of spears. Behind the hedge was a garden. In the garden stood a house like a small castle.

As I was looking up at the turrets and asking myself if there were rooms under them, an old man came and stood next to me.

"Do you like the house?" he asked.

"Yes," I said. "I love the turrets."

"I've lived here for fifty years," he said. "I'm a general, a retired general." He was wearing a shirt and baggy trousers with stripes, not a uniform. That must be because he was retired. He didn't have to wear his uniform any more.

"My father's a soldier," I said, "although he's really a pastry chef. Every day he used to bake twenty different sorts of pastries and three kinds of cakes. But now he has to go around disguised as a bush."

"You know a bit about it then," he said.

"From a book," I said. "I've seen what the inside of a gun looks like, and I know you can get decorations."

"Whose side is your father on?"

"On our side."

"That's good. That means you and I are on the same side, too. Your father is a good man."

"Do you know him?"

"In a manner of speaking."

I didn't know what he meant. "In a manner of speaking" could mean he possibly knew my father, or he certainly knew him, or he certainly wanted to get to know him.

"Are you by yourself?"

What should I say? I was with two women and a man and a boy, but I wasn't allowed to mention them.

"Do you have anything to eat?" he asked.

"Cookies."

"What's your name?"

I told him the name that everyone there could pronounce perfectly well.

"One can't live on cookies," he said. "My wife would enjoy having a child as a guest. And you can have a look in the turrets."

At home I wouldn't be allowed to go anywhere with strangers. But that's exactly what I was doing to get across the border. And this man knew my father. In a manner of speaking. And he had food.

"I'm hungry," I said. "And I don't have any money left."

7

I followed the old man indoors, into a high-ceilinged hallway. A dark red carpet covered the floor. On the wall hung a painting of him when he was young. You could see a little bit of his uniform. The decorations had gold thread.

He called out to his wife. She hurried from the kitchen. She was also very old.

"Look what we have here," he said, holding my shoulders as if he wanted to press me into the carpet.

"A child!" she exclaimed. "Come and put your bag down. Make yourself at home. You must have something to eat and drink."

"Thank you," I said, remembering that this was something I mustn't forget to say.

"Set the table," the retired general told his wife. "While you're doing that, I'll take the child up to see the turret rooms."

The bannister of the wide staircase was decorated with a yawning lion. Once we reached the landing, we had another flight of stairs to climb and then one more. Beneath the roof was a small hallway with four doors. Behind each door was a turret room and in each turret room stood a bed. In one of the rooms the retired general lifted me up high, turning slowly so I could see out the windows in all directions. I saw the trees in the garden. I saw the street with the long wall. I saw a forest spreading out behind the house. And I saw the other three turrets up close.

We went downstairs again. On the second floor the general let me look at his magnificent study. Two enormous chairs stood on either side of a low table. There was also a dark brown writing table. A uniform hung on the wall behind a sheet of glass. It was covered with decorations.

"Sit down," he said, pointing to a chair. He sat in the one opposite.

"You'll have learned all about me, won't you?"

I had no idea what he meant.

"I'm in the school textbooks so you must have studied me, unless you haven't got up to me yet. By rights you ought to know who I am. Come on, who am I? General See…See…Have a guess!"

I'd never learned about a general whose name started with See.

"I've heard of seedlings," I offered. "We were taught about the two sorts of seedlings once." In fact, I could still remember their interesting names: monocotyledons and dicotyledons.

He looked disappointed. He thought I should have known who he was. But there was so much I didn't know. I didn't know what a border looked like. I had no idea how old a hippopotamus could get. I didn't know any famous movie stars. I didn't know where I'd be tomorrow.

"So, didn't you ever learn about the Battle of the Water?"

"Well, in a manner of speaking," I said, since that was probably the sort of thing he wanted to hear.

"That was me! Now you remember! That was me! I was decorated for it."

He stood up, pointing to the decorations sewn onto his old uniform. He went on to explain how he had earned each of them. I listened carefully in case he tested me on them later.

"I received this decoration because I was so good at deceiving the enemy. I'd devised a series of deceptive commands. You see, if you call out 'Attack!' the enemy might hear you and know you plan to attack. Then the enemy thinks, we'll do the same! So, instead, I called out 'Frankfurters!' My men knew that it meant 'Attack!' The enemy, on the other hand, wondered where on earth our soldiers managed to get frankfurters from. Understand?

"And this decoration is for courage, leadership, and loyalty. Because they weren't sure how to represent those, what you see here are a hat, a small tapestry, and a sleeve. Whoever sees it thinks, 'Aha! that's for courage, leadership, and loyalty.'

"And I received this decoration for inventing different kinds of camouflage. You already know something about that. But have a look here and see what sorts of deceptions are possible. Is this camouflage or not?"

He picked up a book from his desk and showed me a couple of pictures.

"And I received this decoration for my bravery. I was never, ever afraid. Are you sometimes scared?"

Yes, I was sometimes. I sat there in that high-ceilinged room with the enormous furniture, feeling smaller and smaller. The retired general was making me scared, but I was too scared to say so out loud.

"I'll test you," he said. "I've devised a comprehensive test to tell how scared someone is because if you're not fearless you're no use to a general, none whatsoever. Is your father brave?"

"I don't know," I mumbled.

"Listen. We'll start with Scary Words, and we'll go on to Scary Pictures, then Unexpected Situations. Now, where's that list of Scary Words? Oh yes, here it is. As I read out the words I'll take your pulse and watch to see if your hands shake and if you get goose bumps and if you find it hard to swallow and if you break out in a cold sweat. Ha, ha. Here's the first word..."

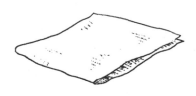

8

"Dinner's ready!" That was the wife of the retired general. She was calling from the foot of the stairs. Relieved, I leaped up and shot downstairs.

She said I had to go to the kitchen with her to wash my hands.

In the kitchen she gave me a bar of soap. She took the towel hanging beside the bench and laid it next to the sink ready for me to use. She kept an eye on me as I washed my hands.

"Not like that," she said. "More thoroughly. Between your fingers."

I rubbed the soapsuds between my fingers, rinsed, and reached for the towel.

"Put the towel back on its hook," she said, once I'd dried my hands.

"No, not that hook, the one next to it. Yes. That one. And straighten the towel, otherwise everything starts to look messy. That's it. Now go to the table."

She pushed me into the dining room. The retired general was already there.

"You deserted," he said severely.

I didn't know what he meant.

"You left without good reason, while we were still busy. We don't do that in this house."

"But dinner was ready," I said.

"And we don't answer back, either!"

I thought I'd better not say anything else.

Steaming pots stood on the table. I sat on the chair
I was told to.

"Don't hold your hands in your lap," said the
general's wife. "That's bad manners. Rest them on
either side of your plate. And pass me your plate so I
can dish up for you."

I had no idea how I was supposed to rest my
hands beside my plate as well as use them to pass
my plate over.

"Come on," she said, "I asked you to do something."

I passed over my plate. She dished up a big piece of meat and a mountain of potatoes and watery vegetables. It was far too much. I was hungry but at the same time it felt as if someone was pushing down on my stomach.

"Now we'll give thanks for our daily bread," she said.

I got a fright. I thought I'd forgotten to say thank you again.

"Thank you for the meal," I said quickly.

"Shhh! Be quiet!"

I saw the retired general and his wife shut their eyes and each placed their right hand over their heart. They mumbled something I didn't understand. Since they weren't looking, I thought I might have time to put a potato back. I stabbed one with my fork, but it was only halfway there when it slipped off and landed on the tablecloth. I picked it up with my fingers and tossed it into the pot. Flaky bits were left on the cloth. My fingers felt burnt.

The general and his wife finished their mumbling.

"What were you doing?" she said. Obviously she hadn't shut her eyes at all. "Were you eating with your fingers? During the prayer? For that you won't have any meat today!"

Using the big meat fork, she transferred my piece back to the pan. I didn't mind. I didn't like the look of the fatty bits round the edges anyway. Now there was just the right amount of food on my plate. I tried to eat it as quietly as I could.

"Lovely meat," said the general, sounding like an advertiser.

His wife looked at me and said, "If you behave yourself, you'll get lovely meat here every day."

"But I'm not staying," I said.

"What did you say?"

"I said I'm not staying. I'm only visiting."

The general's wife coughed and looked at her husband.

"Listen," said the general. "Your father is a soldier. And whereabouts is your mother?"

"On the other side of the border," I said, trailing a snaky piece of cabbage over my plate.

"We know what's going on," said the general. "People either come to this border crossing openly because they have someone to meet them on the other side, or they come secretly and try to cross illegally. What are *you* doing?"

I thought I'd better not say anything. Because our group was planning to cross over secretly in the night.

I said instead, "The two kinds of seedlings are monocotyledons and dicotyledons."

That didn't help, of course.

I saw them look at one another.

"Are you for or against us?" the general asked sternly.

To be on the safe side, I said I was for them. I kept my legs still under the table so I wouldn't kick the general or his wife by accident.

"That's lucky," she said. I could see a fatty piece of meat in her mouth as she spoke.

"Let me make it clear," the general said. "I forbid you to cross the border. You belong here. You're one of us. If you change sides you'll be betraying your own country. And you're part of this country's future."

I wanted to say that I was planning to come back, but I kept quiet.

"Once you cross the border," he said, "you'll never feel completely at home here again."

I hadn't even crossed the border yet, but I already felt that way.

"We've welcomed you with open arms," said his wife, "so you might as well stay here with us. It would be irresponsible of us to let you go."

"But I have to go to my mother," I said.

She suddenly began to shout and mash her potatoes into the plate. "You could show a little thanks! As punishment you can go to bed as soon as you've finished eating."

"Dearest, control yourself," said the general.

"Back me up then," she shouted at him. "You never back me up!"

"That's not true," he said.

"It is true!" she yelled.

"You shouldn't say things like that," he said.

"Don't tell me what to say!" she screamed.

"Then don't tell me off for something I haven't done!" he yelled.

"You're telling *me* off!" she yelled.

"Be quiet!" he yelled.

"You be quiet!" she yelled.

All at once, they both shut up. They looked at me quickly and then stared for ages at the pots.

My stomach was full of homesickness. There was no room for anything else.

9

After dinner, I had to follow the general's wife upstairs. She gave me a nightie that was too big and waited while I got changed.

She wanted to make sure I brushed my teeth properly. She tucked me into bed in one of the turret rooms.

"Everything will be all right." She stroked my hair. I don't like it when people I don't know touch my hair. I didn't say anything back.

Slowly it grew dark outside. I could see the moon and stars. Neither my father nor my grandmother knew I was here. I hoped they were looking up at the moon, too, saying my name, and that they would never stop thinking about me.

The moon disappeared behind a cloud. It became pitch dark.

Soon the people I had travelled with in the car would be crossing the border without me.

That couldn't happen. It must not.

I slipped out of bed. I didn't turn on the light in case I gave myself away.

I felt for my clothes. I hoped I wasn't putting them on inside out. I fished my book and pen out of my bag. I tore out a scrap of paper and, without even seeing the words, wrote on it, "Thank you."

I went quietly down the stairs. Once or twice a tree outside creaked and I stopped and held my breath. On the first floor I heard two people snoring, one loudly, the other softly.

On the ground floor, I groped my way to the front door. I couldn't unlock it. I tried the back door in the kitchen but I couldn't open that either. I tried the window beside it. I had better luck with that.

As I crawled out, I knocked over the glasses that were on the windowsill. I'd noticed them earlier when I washed my hands. Now they smashed onto the floor.

I ran blindly away from the little castle. I trampled flowers as I went and then I blundered into a hedge.

Luckily I found the gate that led onto the street. It wasn't locked.

What was the number above the door in the wall? Was it nine? No, number nine didn't open. Neither did number eight.

Just as I reached number seven, a hushed group of people came out. They didn't see me because I was hidden by the open door. Leading them was a man I hadn't seen before. It wasn't the driver. Perhaps it was his brother or a friend, someone who wanted a share in the money we had handed over. He would have to do something to earn it, of course.

I recognized the two sighing women. I had arrived in the nick of time. It was a relief to join them again.

"I was almost too late," I whispered.

"Shhh!" hissed the women. "We must be absolutely silent."

A path between two hedges ran alongside the retired general's garden and led to the forest.

I saw lights on the first floor of the little castle. They had woken up. Probably because they had heard the glasses crash onto the floor. We had to hurry, I thought in panic. They'd better not catch up with us because I'd deserted.

We followed one another in a line. Once or twice I had to run to keep up. It was pitch dark in the forest.

I didn't speak. I wanted to but we weren't allowed. I wanted to say that my father was hidden in another forest. I wanted to ask why borders were called borders and who had invented them, and what would happen if someone decided to put a border exactly where people were living. Would they belong in both places or in neither?

Sometimes tracer fire shot across the sky. Whenever that happened we had to lie on the ground. The earth was damp and the cold soaked into my clothes. At times like that, I felt as if I hardly existed anymore.

We went on walking through the forest, over dead leaves, between bushes and through a ditch. My eyes grew used to the dark. Sometimes I got a fright, thinking I saw a wolf, but it would only be a branch that looked like a wolf.

My leg got caught as we scrambled over a tree trunk. My left shoe came off amongst the fallen branches. I couldn't call out for the others to wait because I wasn't meant to make a sound. I had to behave as if I wasn't there, but now I *really* wasn't there. They carried on without noticing. They probably thought I was doing my best to be inconspicuous. They didn't know me at all, not even my name.

I tugged my leg free and scrabbled on the ground until I found my shoe. I stumbled along on my own. If there were tracer fire in the sky it would be easier to tell where the border was, I thought, because it would be coming from that direction. But then I'd have to throw myself down again, and you can't see much with your face to the ground.

After a while the moon peeped out again. I saw it through the trees, doing its best for me. It helped. It helped so much that I could see a small house not far away.

It turned out to be only an old hut, but as far as I was concerned it was a house where I could sleep.

The sagging door groaned as I opened it. It gave me such a fright, I threw myself onto the ground again. But nothing bad happened. The door stayed open as if to say, Are you coming inside or what?

In the morning, when it was light, I'd disguise myself as a bush and shuffle carefully to the border, making bird sounds every now and then.

It was pitch dark in the hut. I felt planks of wood and spiderwebs. I lay down behind a few of the planks. My bag became my pillow. The cookies crumbled under my head.

My father and grandmother knew I existed. They would let me wander around in their thoughts. I wondered if they said "good night" into the air each evening and made sure they kept their arms warm for me to come back to.

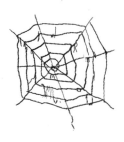

10

Just as I was falling asleep, I heard footsteps. Twigs snapped. The door of the hut groaned. I rolled further away and stayed as stiff as a plank. A plank with shoes on.

Someone shone a pocket flashlight onto the floor. Through a gap in the planks I saw a pair of soldier's boots. I didn't know if the boots belonged to our side or the other one.

Suddenly my whole body began to shake. I couldn't help it. My brain tried to tell my skin and muscles and nerves to behave normally, but they took no notice. My legs trembled.

"Who's there?" hissed the man in the soldier's boots. I could tell from his voice that he was scared, too.

I said softly, "Nobody."

"I'm nobody as well," the man whispered, shining his flashlight in my direction. "Where did you come from?"

"From nowhere," I whispered back.

"May I come inside?"

"Nobody's allowed inside."

"Good," I heard him say. "That means I'm allowed."

He shone his light on my shoes and bent down to see what sort of person was attached to them.

The spiderwebs were lit up. There were no spiders living in them.

"You're just a girl," he said, sounding friendly.

I was no longer shaking.

"Are you here alone? Have you lost your parents? Come on out. I'm not going to hurt you."

He shifted the planks I was hiding behind and shone the light in my face. I squeezed my eyes shut. Then he shone the flashlight at his own face, aiming at his forehead. If he had held it under his chin, he would have looked really spooky. I saw a grimy face, a grin, and sad, doggy eyes. His uniform was grubby and torn and he wasn't wearing a single decoration. I couldn't see a rifle or gun either. Perhaps he'd left them behind in the forest.

He sat down on the floor.

I sat up across from him. We talked to each other, very quietly, no louder than the murmur of trees around the hut.

"Are you on the run as well?" he asked.

"I'm on the way to my mother's place," I said. "But I've gone and lost the people who were taking me across the border."

"That's where I'm heading, too," he said. "They're after me because I've failed in courage, leadership, and loyalty."

I asked him how that happened.

"I'm a captain, a commanding officer," he said. "When there was no war I seemed to be good at it. But once war came, it turned out I was no good at all."

"What did you do wrong?"

"I couldn't command," he said. "When I had to call out, 'Open fire!' I said instead, 'Perhaps we should try shooting now, as long as it's not too dangerous and not too much trouble for anyone.' But my men didn't hear because I spoke too softly, and they started shooting at random. That ended miserably, of course, and it was my fault. And when I had to shout, 'Forward, march!' I said instead, 'Would you mind walking on a little further, please?' And then my men had no idea where to go. They stumbled about and fell over each other. They yelled that they might as well command themselves, and they all started giving orders at the same time. One roared for them to go straight ahead, another for them to go left, and another right.

"One ordered them to attack, another to hunt for cover. And through all that, I called out, 'Listen boys, why don't we come to some sort of compromise?' But they had no idea what I meant, and then everything went wrong. My soldiers ended up running all over the place trying to chase down the enemy. And that's why they're after me now. Because I haven't shown courage, leadership, and loyalty. They'll punish me when they find me. You won't give me away, will you?"

"Never," I said.

I had no idea what he had meant by "compromise," but I didn't ask.

"Do you want a crumbled cookie?" I asked. "And a drink of water?" I passed him my bottle and the least-broken cookie. Four chunks and two fat crumbs. I could tell he was very happy with them. He probably hadn't had anything to eat or drink for ages.

"I didn't know giving orders was so hard," I said. "Most people are good at it. They say, 'Sit still' or 'Be quiet' or 'Hurry up' or 'Go and play somewhere else' and things like that."

"Yes, I thought I could do that, too," the captain sighed. "But once it was for real, I discovered I couldn't."

"Some things I can't do very well either," I said to cheer him up. "For instance, I'm no good at drawing a sugar bowl. And I baked some cookies once that grew into one big slab in the oven, so you couldn't tell where one cookie finished and the next one began."

"The more you practice, the better you'll get," he said.

"But that's the same for you. Why don't you practice now? You can practice on me."

"What should I say?"

"Try saying, 'Move over' and then I'll move over."

"Okay, I'll do that. Would you mind…Oh, no, not that way. I have to draw out the first word and emphasise the next bit. But, given the circumstances, not too loudly. Here goes: Mooooooove…*over!*"

Although he said "over" quietly, it sounded like a real command. I moved over, telling him how well he had done and that he could practice on me some more.

He thought of some new orders.

He whispered: "Pinnnnnnnch your *nose*," and I pinched my nose.

"Shaaaaake your *foot*," and I shook my foot.

"Poiiiiiint to the *floor*," and I pointed to the floor.

He could do it. And while we were so busy, he seemed to forget why he was in the hut.

But suddenly he remembered.

"It'll be light soon," he whispered. "It might be best if we stay hidden until tonight. Then we'll try to get to the border. We have to follow the pole star. That's a bright star. And we have to be able to hide if necessary."

"I don't know which star the pole star is," I said.

"I'll point it out now, but we'll have to make sure the coast is clear."

We crept out of the hut. The door groaned again. As we pressed ourselves against the outside wall, he pointed up at an angle. I saw the starry sky between the trees.

"There," he whispered, "that big one is the pole star. At night all the stars move except for the pole star. Come on, back inside now."

"But I have to pee," I said.

"Quickly then, go and hide. And be careful."

I crept between two bushes and peed. Any little creatures crawling on the ground must have been drenched by the sudden downpour.

As I pulled my jeans up again, I heard twigs snapping. I clearly heard the rhythm of footsteps. There were people out there, but I didn't know what sort of people. I must not move. I must not give myself or the captain away. I was too scared to zip up my jeans. I hardly dared to breathe.

Between the leaves I saw a terrible sight. Three men in uniform with rifles over their shoulders. They were heading straight for the hut. The first two can't have known where the doorknob was. They kicked down the door with their boots and marched into the hut. I heard them yell but couldn't tell what. This was the moment for the captain to shout: "Geeeet *out! Aaaat once!*" We'd practiced it so well. But I didn't hear him.

Soon afterwards the two men came outside with the captain between them. They held onto him so hard, he had no chance of getting away. The third man, who had stayed on guard outside, followed them with his rifle at the ready. The captain looked round in case he could see me.

I wanted to shout after him, "I didn't give you away! I'd never have given you away!"

But I didn't say anything.

I watched him go and nothing in the world made any sense.

11

I didn't dare go back to the hut. And I missed the captain. We were going to cross the border together.

Now he might think that I couldn't be trusted. Perhaps he would never trust anyone again.

I missed my father who was in another forest somewhere. And I missed my grandmother who was protecting our house from intruders.

My bag was still in the hut. But because it was starting to get light it was better to stay hidden in the bushes until it was dark again. That would take a long time. And I had no food or drink with me.

I wanted to lie down but not in my own pee. Carefully, I shuffled a little way away. The ground was damp and chilly, but at least I could lie down, hidden from the world. And it wasn't raining. And there were no earthquakes or floods.

I fell asleep and dreamed that the captain was giving urgent orders: "Don't take me away! Do something!" I kept wailing, "I can't get to you, I can't reach you!"

When I woke up, it was daylight but I had no idea what the time was. I sat up. It had become warm. The ground was dappled with sunlight. I heard the rustlings of what must have been birds and small animals all around me. They were also staying well hidden.

I never knew that half a day could last so long when you had nothing to do except wait for it to be over. Giving my brain something to do helped. I put all sorts of things into lists. My favorite foods, for example. At the top of the list were my father's pastries. All twenty sorts came first equal. Then I carried on to number ten. Next I started on the streets near our house, listing them by name. After that I went on to classmates: those I liked the best and those who were the most irritating, and those who came in between. I listed things in alphabetical order. Ape, bear, chihuahua, dromedary, right through to zebra. If I didn't know an animal, I made one up. I also made up an alphabetical list of words that, as far as I knew, didn't mean anything. Appen, bleer, candrow, dilk…

That's how I tried to get through the day. My mouth dried out and my stomach rumbled.

When night finally came, I slipped back to the hut, giving my eyes time to get used to the dark.

The captain hadn't put up a fight. He hadn't thrown any planks at the two men to try and defend himself. His flashlight still lay on the floor. I turned it on briefly to see where my bag was. It was tucked away in a corner. I noticed something else on the ground. A small plastic bag.

I hid behind a pile of planks so no one could see the light from outside. I opened the bag. Inside was a photo of the captain and his wife and a little girl.

Stuck to the photo was a letter from someone who couldn't write properly yet. It must have been from his daughter.

I put the letter and the photo in my notebook. As soon as I got the chance, I would write to his wife and daughter. I'd tell them how he showed me the pole star and how I saw him being taken away. And also how we'd been planning to travel on together until he was safe.

I was about to shut the notebook when I suddenly noticed I'd made a big mistake. At the retired general's place, when I'd torn off a scrap of paper in the dark and written "Thank you" on it, I'd accidentally torn the piece from the page with my mother's address on it. All I had left was the name of the town where she lived. Her street and the number of her house were back at the little castle. And one town has a lot of streets.

I ate five broken cookies, had three drinks of water, and threw the notebook and the flashlight into my bag. Now that it was dark, I had to try to cross the border.

Outside, I looked up between the trees for the pole star that would be my guide. I moved from bush to bush like a night animal. I kept my ears pricked for any suspicious sounds. The pole star stayed in the same place and led me on. I just hoped the border wasn't a wide river, or made of barbed wire.

I don't know how long I walked and wove my way through the forest but at last I saw light in the distance. When I got closer I saw that it came from streetlights. I had arrived in a silent town. People were asleep inside their houses. Only a cat was awake and looking at me curiously. In the lamplight I could read what was written on the shop windows. One shop had sausages and hams on display as well as a stuffed and mounted sheep.

Slasselerie it said. That was like our word for butcher's shop, but not the same. I must have crossed the border without even realizing it. The trees and bushes had stayed exactly the same, and I had seen no line on the ground, no gate or trench, or tracer fire.

To make sure, I had a look at other shops in case the butcher was no good at spelling. But they all had the other language written on them. It said *Wisselerie* on the fish shop and *Drouzelerie* on the clothes shop window. If I hadn't seen a poster of fish, and clothes hanging on racks, I wouldn't have known what either of the shops was selling.

Every door in the village was shut. I had no idea where to go. So I sat down on a doorstep to wait for daybreak.

A man delivering newspapers walked past. He looked at me without saying anything. But he probably thought to himself, What's that child doing there? She should be in bed, not in a doorway.

I think he went and told the police because soon afterwards a car stopped right in front of me. Two policemen were in it. They must have had to get up as early as my father used to when he baked pastries. One of them asked, "Woe doensel joe dor?"

I understood that. Slowly and carefully I explained in my own language that I had crossed the border and was on the way to my mother's. He seemed to understand and replied, "Oe bringsel joe."

I had to go with them. The sky had started to lighten as we drove out of town, past fields that looked exactly the same as ours.

The car stopped in front of a big building. It was surrounded by a high fence with cameras above the entrance gates.

I found myself in a hallway with a counter behind an open, sliding window. The policemen left me in front of it.

The man behind the counter could speak my language, even though he used a word or two from his own. He asked me if I had any papers. I showed him my notebook. At first he said that wasn't what he had meant but then he saw the copy of my father's passport, which had my name in it.

He said that my name with its four *k*'s was impossible to pronounce. They didn't have that letter in their language. He'd get tongue-tied trying to say it. It would be better if I just used the last four letters of my first name: toda. I had to be called Toda here.

"Otherwise you won't get anywhere," he said.

Then he pointed to a door. I had to go through it and wait my turn.

I wondered why I wouldn't get anywhere using my real name. My mother wouldn't know who I was if I started using another name. And my father and grandmother never had any trouble saying my name. It was as if my legs still had a name, but my head and arms no longer did.

12

A lot of people sat in the waiting room. The two women, the man, and the boy weren't there. Everybody looked tired. Perhaps they'd all been waiting a long time. They might not have worked out that you can make time go faster by listing things in your head. But perhaps their heads were too tired or too full of worries to handle lists. My head was full of worries, too, but there was still room for other thoughts. For instance, I wondered if I was allowed to have any of the food and drink I could see on a table in the corner. I wondered if I should help myself. One of the other people seemed to be able to read my mind.

"Yes, you can help yourself," he said in my language.

I heard more people speaking my language. They must have crossed the border, too. I felt like asking them if they had actually seen the border and what it looked like, but I didn't.

There were bread rolls in plastic bags. The bags were very hard to open, especially since I was nervous. Perhaps they'd used those bags on purpose so you had something to do while you were waiting. First I tried opening one with my hands, and then with my teeth. The bag suddenly burst open and my bread roll fell onto the floor. I picked it up and brushed it as clean as I could. I didn't dare take another one. That would look ungrateful.

On the table there were also plastic cups with lids. They only had water in them. But the cups were nicely decorated with a landscape. If this country was like the picture on the cup, then it was a beautiful place.

From time to time someone came in and pointed at one of the people waiting. He or she then had to go with them.

When it was my turn, I followed a woman to a room with a table and two hard chairs. Behind a computer sat a man who spoke my language, even though he pronounced all the *k*'s with an accent.

"We need you to answer a few questions," he said. "So sit down. First question. Are you useful?"

I didn't understand the first question at all but I

didn't know if I should say so. This might be a sort of test and later on he would say, What a pity, four mistakes and you're only allowed two. Your time is up. You have to go back to where you came from.

"Are you useful?" he asked again.

In the end I said, "I don't know how I'm supposed to answer."

"What can you do that will benefit this country?" he asked me.

I could to do a lot of things, but would they be any good for this country? I could cook eggs. I could recite the seventeen-times table. I could name all the streets in my neighbourhood.

"I can arrange hair in different ways," I said. "And I can pretend to be a tree. That's good for tricking the enemy."

"Have you been to school?" he asked.

"Yes," I said. "I was going to school."

"What's eight times thirteen?"

"One hundred and four."

"Good. And which battle was fought in the Third Supremacy Struggle?"

I only knew the name of one battle so I said it. "The Battle of the Water."

"Good," he said. "So you do know something. Now for some other questions. How did you get across the border?"

"I don't know," I said, "because I didn't see where it was."

But he meant something else.

"Did you come by yourself? Do you have any family here?"

"Yes," I said. "My mother. I know which town she lives in, but I don't have her address anymore."

I had to write down the name of the town and my mother's name. He spent ages looking at his computer screen. Then he said he couldn't find anyone with that name. That gave me a terrible shock. I had to find her.

"I had her address to start with," I said, "but I left it with the retired general by mistake."

"So you're saying that your mother lives here and you don't?"

"Yes," I said. "My mother's been here since I was very little."

The man typed away busily on his keyboard. I suppose he had to record everything I said so that later on he could say to me, See, this is what you told me. After all, it's impossible to remember everything you've said unless you've written it down.

I just hoped he had written down exactly what I had said. Because if you don't understand something properly, then there's a chance you could write it down wrongly as well. Someone could say, "My mama's here" and someone else might think they said, "My gum is clear" or "My bum is bare."

Suddenly the man said, "You're not telling the truth, are you. You're just making things up."

"But I'm not!" I cried out in fright. "I'm telling the truth!"

"And obviously the reason you're making such a fuss now is because you don't believe any of it yourself."

My whole head became hot with anger.

"I *am* telling the truth," I repeated in a quieter voice. "My grandmother wrote down the address but I accidentally used it to write 'Thank you' on."

"You're blushing," he said. "People do that when they're hiding something."

Now I began to cry. I tried to hold back the tears by thinking of nice things. Like my father's pastries. Or my grandmother's hair. Or the pole star. But nothing worked.

The man told me not to snivel, otherwise he wouldn't be able to understand what I was saying.

"Is your grandmother here?"

"No," I sniffed, "She's at home."

"Where's your father? Is he away fighting?"

I'd never thought of my father as someone who was fighting. I had only thought of him as someone who was hidden by camouflage. I knew he hated fighting. He couldn't even stand being tickled.

"I started off by bus," I said. "I lost the others."

"And why should I believe you?"

"Because it's true!"

"Then tell me the color of your mother's eyes."

"I don't know," I said. "Because I haven't seen her since she left. And her photo is in black and white."

"You're clever," he said. "Clever enough to invent an answer. What was the name of the street where you lived?"

Of course I knew that.

"And what color was your house?"

That was a harder question to answer.

"It was painted," I said, "but not just an ordinary color. In some places it was the color of eggshell but in other places it was like some of my father's pastries, sand colored, but browner and a little bit grainy, and once someone wrote something on the wall that I couldn't read and then we had to..."

"Enough, enough."

He began to shuffle papers around and fiddle with his fingernails. He seemed to have forgotten I was there.

When he looked at me again, he said, "There's a Child Welfare Center in the town where you say your mother lives. I'll see if I can get you in there. But you'll have to tell them the truth."

"Can I ring my grandmother from here?" I asked.

"No, miss, you can't. No calls are possible at the moment. The services are down where your grandmother lives."

He stood up and came towards me. I thought he was coming to shake hands so I held mine out. But that wasn't it. He had only got up to stick a number on my sleeve.

"That's your number," he said. "It's provisional. Go back to the waiting room now. Someone will come and get you when it's time for your examination."

It was only when I returned the waiting room that I noticed that lots of other people had numbers on their sleeves.

"The services are down at home," I said to number 459156, who was sitting beside me.

"Well, what did you expect?" He got up and walked over to the door as if he couldn't care less what I thought or said.

021230

13

Not long afterwards someone else came to pluck me from the waiting room. It was a young woman in a white apron.

"Joe moesel beziensel wurre," she said.

I supposed it was my turn for an examination. But first I had to have a shower. She wanted to know if I had clean clothes with me. She pointed out the shower. I had to put a plastic token into a slot before any water would come out. There wasn't much water and it didn't last for long. I was still covered in soap when it stopped. I wiped the soap off with a thin facecloth and put on clean clothes. They still smelled of the forest, and there were crumbs in the folds.

The young woman took me to another room. First she took a photo of my head and shoulders. Then I had to put my index finger onto an inkpad. She used my finger as a stamp. Why hadn't she done that before the shower? Now I had a blue finger.

An older woman in a white coat came from behind her desk and told me to undress. And I had only just put my clothes on. I even had to pull down my underwear for a moment. That was worse than anything at school or in the General Welfare building.

The woman checked me all over. She tapped and pressed and listened, making sure that everything inside me was working properly.

Then I had to lie down on a high bed. She wanted

to measure me. She measured how wide my eyes were. I had to smile while she measured my lips, then pretend I'd eaten a lemon while she measured them again. She compared my ears, hissing "Pffll" in one ear and then "Pffll" in the other.

"Woe hiebsel jeheur?" she asked me. I thought she wanted me to tell her what I could hear.

"Pffllpfflloehiebseljeheur," I said.

"Heu bedeusel joe?" she asked.

"Heubedeuseljoe," I replied.

She looked angrily at me. Perhaps her job would have been more interesting if I hadn't been able to hear.

She pushed down on my skin and pulled my arms, as if to see whether they would come off. She measured the depth of my belly button with a little fishing rod.

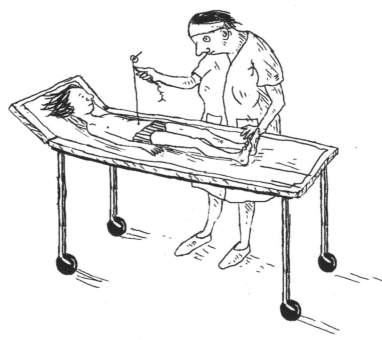

I had to turn over onto my stomach. She pinched my neck and my bottom and tickled the soles of my feet. After that I had to stand up again.

"Jasel nor die doersel," she said, pointing at the door. I walked towards the door.

"Jasel wiedrum nor meu," she said, pointing at herself. I walked back towards her.

"Noe wiedrum nor die doersel."

I was almost back at the door when she suddenly screamed "AAAAA!"

I got such a fright, I threw myself to the floor.

"Brima rejafsievermeusel," she said.

I didn't think much of her reflex test. It had suddenly reminded me of the blasts I'd heard when I slept in the bakery with my grandmother.

At last I was allowed to put the rest of my clothes back on. But I hadn't finished yet.

An interpreter who understood my language came in and sat behind the desk. The woman in the white coat sat beside him. The interpreter began asking me lots more questions while the woman filled in forms. I had to answer yes or no.

"Have you ever broken anything?" the interpreter asked.

"Yes," I said.

"Was it a leg?"

"No," I said.

"Was it an arm?"

"No," I said, "it was my father's best mug."

"That's not what we mean," said the interpreter.

"We mean any part of your body."

"Yes, my fingernails."

"Is that all?"

"Yes."

"Next question. Have you ever had pimples with red tops?"

"No."

"Purple bruises?"

"Yes."

"I'm going to name some illnesses. Answer yes or no if you've had any of them. The illness of Johan Peter Alexander Von Der Houpst, the yellow-pimple disease, the sickness that could be one thing or another, the reverse flu, knocking knees, the drizzles, gray melancholy..."

The long list of illnesses went on and on. I answered no, no, no. The interpreter also asked if I had any trouble going. I had no idea what he meant. It turned out he meant did I have any trouble with peeing or pooping.

"Yes," I said. "There was no bathroom in the forest and I don't know where the bathroom here is."

The two people behind their desk were becoming impatient. I had already decided I wasn't going to be impatient anymore. After all, I had managed to spend a whole day hiding in the bushes.

The woman in the white coat still had my throat to look at because she'd forgotten to do that before. She started exactly as I was about to say something. It seemed as if she was looking for my words, behind my teeth and under my tongue. By the time she finished, I'd forgotten what they were.

Someone else came to collect me. A bus was waiting outside. I had to get on board right away. The bus was already almost full.

Before I knew what was happening, we were driving out through the high gates. No one told me where they were taking me. The bus stopped several times at different buildings and each time people got off.

I was the last one. The driver gestured that we had at least four more hours to go. I fell asleep and didn't wake up until it was time for me to get off.

I hadn't even seen whether the countryside here was as beautiful as it was on the cups in the waiting room.

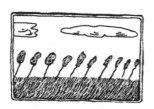

14

The Child Welfare Center stood well back from the street. You had to go through a gate and down an alleyway between two houses, then you entered a courtyard and there it was.

Thirteen other children lived there. Some had crossed the border like me. But most of them hadn't. They thought the way I talked was strange. They said, "Woe brassel die roreslig!"

I was given a room of my own. It was so small that it could only fit a bed and a stool. But I had a view of the garden.

I had arrived too late for dinner so I had to sit by myself at a long table and eat a snack. A couple of kids watched me out of curiosity. Maybe they thought that someone from another country would eat differently. But I didn't.

A woman with spiky hair came to get me for bed. She pointed out the bathroom, gave me a clean towel, and told me to get a good rest. In the morning we'd see what was what.

I lay awake for a long time. There were so many sounds around me and I didn't know yet where they came from. I felt like a package that had been delivered to the wrong address.

When I finally got to sleep, I dreamed I was home again. Our house was around the corner from the Child Welfare Center. My grandmother said she felt so hot she could hardly breathe. Out of the blue, my mother was there as well. I asked her why she had suddenly turned up. I didn't understand her reply, and then she started laughing. I went into the garden and my father was there, disguised as a bush. I told him he didn't need to be a bush anymore. He could go back to being normal. So he began to pull the branches and leaves off himself, but other ones grew in their place. "They'll never come off!" he shouted. "They'll never come off!"

The woman with the spiky hair shook me awake. She said I had to get up and have some breakfast. She told me to hurry because the other children were already up.

I washed only my hands and face and then got dressed quickly. There was still a number on my sleeve.

The noise of the other children led me back to the dining room.

I hoped they wouldn't want to keep me here. I hoped someone had explained to them, This one is going to her mother. She doesn't have to stay.

The children around me spoke so quickly that I couldn't follow a word they said. They laughed, but I didn't know why. Sometimes they wouldn't look at me and seemed to be talking about me. That made me feel uncomfortable.

After breakfast I had to go to a small office. The woman with the spiky hair could speak my language a bit. Sometimes she said a word wrongly. She asked, "Are you looking for your modder?" But I knew she meant mother.

She told me I would have to stay at the Center until my mother had been found. But she didn't say who was going to look for her or whether they would do their very best. I wasn't sure if she believed that my mother actually lived here.

She said I might as well start learning the language of my new country.

She gave me two books that I was allowed to keep.

The first book had pictures with matching words underneath. There were also examples of sentences you could use when you were talking to someone.

BRASSELE SPEAK

oe brassel
joe brassel
ieje brassel
noeje brassel
woeje brassel
wieje brassel

oe hiebsel jebras

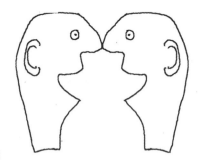

HIEBSELE HAVE

oe hiebsel
joe hiebsel
ieje heubs
noeje hiebsel
woeje hiebsel
wieje heubs

oe hiebsel jeheub

SINSELE BE

oe sinsel
joe sedde
ieje wees
noeje sinsel
woeje sedde
wieje wees

oe hiebsel jewees

Oewe sedde joe?
How are you?

Brallewozewie, wide!
Fine, thanks!

Hoedeloe! Boe noeje sinsel hirre?
Hello! Where are we?

Oe drawsel meu pieselie brezensele?
May I introduce myself?

Wiesel joe boe wees mjamjam?
Do you know where the restaurant is?

Wiesel joe hirre slaberie?
Can you recommend a hotel?

Zorseloor?
I'm sorry!

Oe nienofsel znabsel.
I don't understand.

Hadsel joe brassele slomster?
Can you speak more slowly?

The second book explained the things that were done differently here than in my country.

For instance, what was polite and what wasn't. And what you should say and take with you if you were invited out for a meal.

ETIQUETTE
Oewe heursel die feddeling

1. The right expressions:
    Dajjebedangsel - *Thank you*
    Blesirie jedoen - *You're welcome*
    Jasel joe - *You go ahead*
    Disnings - *It was no trouble*

2. When speaking with someone you don't know, it is polite to look at the nose, between the person's eyes. You should only look someone right in the eyes if you know them.

3. When visiting, it is best not to bring cut flowers. Your host or hostess would much prefer it if you brought a bag of sugar, a fruit basket, or a homemade napkin ring.

4. On public transport it is not customary to

I learned the examples by heart. As I walked down the hall, I would say to myself, "Wiesel joe boe wees mjamjam?" Or I would say to the woman with the spiky hair, "Oe drawsel meu pieselie brezensele?" Then she would reply that she already knew who I was. But in fact she only knew the tail end of my name.

After a week, still nobody knew where my mother lived. And my mother clearly didn't know that I was living at the Center. I was scared that I'd have to stay there without her ever knowing. And without being able to phone my grandmother and my father to tell them. Because the services were down. Maybe my father didn't know where he was right now, either, or when he would be able to come home.

15

I made a plan. It was a plan to spread messages all over town. I would write on the notes: Does anyone know where my mother lives? And I would add her name. I was able to translate the note by myself, using the book I'd been given.

Weje wiesel boe wees meu mamselie husel?

In my room I pulled out all the empty pages from my notebook. I tore them into quarters and wrote my message on each one. But there weren't enough.

So I took a roll of toilet paper from the bathroom. I unrolled it and wrote my mother's name on each section. When I was finished, a twisty trail of toilet paper covered the bed. I carefully rolled it up again.

I stuffed everything into my bag, and hoped no one would notice me going. It wasn't easy. We weren't allowed out by ourselves unless we had permission. Otherwise we'd be punished.

But I managed. I sneaked down the alleyway between the houses and managed to open the gate onto the street. I thought an alarm might go off when I opened it. I raced along the street and into a side street where I hid in a porch until I got my breath again.

Four streets further on I began to carry out my plan. I hung the messages on branches and laid them on walls. I dropped them into shopping carts and bags when no one was looking, and pushed them into mailboxes in the long rows of front doors.

I didn't have enough messages.

The town was too big.

After I had got rid of them all, I sat down in a bus shelter to rest. But I didn't rest for long because I had a sudden thought that made me jump up.

I had made a mistake in the messages!

I had forgotten to write my own name on them.

And that I was in the Child Welfare Center!

Even if someone knew where my mother was, how could they possibly tell me?

I decided to go back and add my name and where I was living to all the letters I could find.

There were a few that hadn't blown off a wall. The ones on the branches were still there probably because no one had spotted them. Some drifted about in empty shopping carts. I was even able to fish some out of front-door mailboxes, but those were the hardest to get. If I wasn't careful my hand would get caught in a slot.

"Woe doensel joe dor?"

I looked up to see a policewoman.

"Nothing," I said, frightened.

"Joe wisselsel bostsels uiwe i briewzelboesel! Da ies strawwelbiuer!"

She pulled me to my feet. I understood that I had to go with her.

The police station was just around the corner. On the way there I saw a few more of my letters fluttering in the breeze, without my name.

I wanted to say that I had only been trying to find my mother, but the policewoman didn't understand me very well. She said I'd better believe that she would tell my parents what I'd been up to.

At first I just had to wait, but I didn't mind that. There was a large map of the town hanging on the wall in the police station. I was hoping I'd remember the name of my mother's street if I saw it. But I didn't.

Then, in a plain little room smelling of rotten fruit, I had to explain to another policewoman why I'd had my hand in people's private mailboxes. An interpreter arrived to translate the questions and answers. I told them that I was trying to find my mother, and what she was called. And that in the dark I had torn out the name of her street from my notebook so that I could write thank you on it.

At first the policewoman looked for my mother's name in the telephone book and on the internet, but it wasn't there. Then she emptied my bag. There were still dirty underpants and broken cookies inside. She took out my notebook. It had become very thin.

The photo of my father was still inside.

And the crossed-out drawings my grandmother had made of her face.

And the list of things I wanted to remember from home.

And the photo of my mother.

She asked something which the interpreter translated.

"Is this the mother you're looking for?"

It sounded as if I had a whole lot of mothers to choose from.

I nodded, yes.

The police officer left the room, taking my notebook with her. I hoped she'd give it back, because it was mine.

The interpreter began speaking to me again. He asked which side my father was on. I said I didn't know. But that he was really a pastry chef and could make twenty different kinds of pastries. And that he had done that every morning while most other people were still fast asleep.

"The pastries here aren't as good as ours," said the interpreter.

"But there's no war here," I said.

"That's true," he said.

"I can already say, 'Hello! Where are we?'" I said. And I said it, "Hoedeloe! Boe noeje sinsel hirre?"

"Excellent," said the interpreter. "You're a quick learner."

We practiced lots of useful expressions.

Then the police officer returned. The interpreter translated what she told him. "We found your mother's address."

When my grandmother wrote the address in my notebook she had pushed down hard with her pen. That meant the address had pressed itself onto the next page, the page with the list of things I wanted to remember. The police had managed to make the thin, ghostly text readable. And because my mother wasn't in the phone book or on the internet, they'd called her neighbors downstairs. Through them they found my mother.

"And she's on her way here," said the interpreter.

I was very relieved that my mother had been found, but I was also worried that she had to collect me from a police station. She might think that my father had brought me up badly.

Half an hour later she arrived, flustered and perspiring. I recognized her right away, even though she had more wrinkles than in her photo. I didn't feel very used to her though, so I looked at her nose rather than right in her eyes. I thought she wouldn't be offended because she had lived here long enough to know their customs. It wasn't the same as being with my father. My mother hadn't seen me for such a long time. I might look very different from what she had imagined and it would take her a while to get used to the real me.

She gave me three sloppy kisses.

As I looked at her, I missed my father and Gran. Not that I said so out loud.

My mother spoke both languages. She understood everything that the police officer said.

Before we left, we had to write down my new address.

It was a provisional address.

Yes, I understood that.

I would eventually go back home.

The number was taken off my sleeve and put into a small plastic bag. I didn't have to wear it anymore. I belonged here now.

And after that my mother took me to a house I didn't know, but where I had to learn to feel at home. That's what she said to me, first in our own language and then in the language I had to learn.

"Woelsel joe tuzel, misselie, woelsel joe tuzel."

16

And that is how I came to live with my mother for the first time. I felt like a guest. She was happy that I was there. Maybe she had missed me all those years as much as I missed my father and grandmother now.

She had prepared a room for me. My very own room, she said. She had hung up a photo of my other home. A photo of the front showing not only the color of eggshell but also the color of the pastries my father made. The first time we had a cup of tea together, my mother put out two pastries that looked like the ones my father baked, only a bit crooked. She had made them herself. On purpose, so that a bit of him was there, too, even though he wasn't there.

And she had another surprise for me. One letter from my grandmother and another from my dad.

My dearest girl,
Did you arrive safely? I found it so hard to let you go, but it was for the best. Do you still remember all the things we were going to remember?

Hugs and kisses!

Gran

FIELD ARMY, 3RD COMPANY, 1ST BATTALION, 5TH
REGIMENT, 3RD TENT TO THE LEFT.

SWEETHEART,

IF EVERYTHING HAS WORKED OUT, YOU'LL BE
WITH YOUR MOTHER NOW. SHE'LL LOOK AFTER
YOU REALLY WELL. I THINK ABOUT YOU EVERY
DAY! DON'T WORRY ABOUT ME. I'M JUST HAPPY
THAT YOU'RE FAR AWAY FROM THE WAR. AS
SOON AS I CAN, I'LL COME AND GET YOU. AND
I'LL BAKE LOVELY PASTRIES FOR YOU. TELL YOUR
MOTHER THAT IN FUTURE WE'LL DO THINGS
DIFFERENTLY. IF SHE WANTS TO SEE YOU, SHE'LL
BE ABLE TO COME TO OUR PLACE. BEFORE,
THAT WAS A LITTLE TOO DIFFICULT. DO YOU
THINK THAT'S A GOOD IDEA?
I'M LOOKING FORWARD TO THE DAY WHEN I CAN
GIVE YOU A BIG HUG AGAIN. DO YOUR BEST!

LOVE AND KISSES FROM DAD.

How did those letters get here? When they said that the services were down at home, I thought they meant that everything was broken. That water didn't come out of the faucets anymore and that all the mailboxes were ruined and there was nowhere to mail letters. But perhaps not all the services had been down.

I told my mother nearly everything that had happened to me. I showed her the photo that belonged to the captain. Together we wrote a letter to his wife and daughter. We wrote how he had helped me to find the invisible border by following the pole star. And that it was better for him to become something different if that was still possible.

I live with my mother now. And I'll stay here until one side or the other stops fighting. I'll stay here until my father no longer has to be a bush.